Drake's Special Delivery

by Karen Wallace

Illustrated by Jane Cope

W
FRANKLIN WATTS
LONDON·SYDNEY

The Characters

Sydney Woodshavings

Sir Francis Drake

Mary Marchbank

The Monkey

Matilda, Lady Mouthwater

Queen Elizabeth

Toby Crumble

Earl Inkblot

Greedy Gonzalez

Ma Knucklebone

At the Court of Queen Elizabeth

Drake's Special Delivery

by Karen Wallace

Illustrated by Jane Cope

W
FRANKLIN WATTS
LONDON•SYDNEY

First published in 2001 by Franklin Watts
96 Leonard Street, London EC2A 4XD

Editor: Louise John
Designer: Jason Anscomb
Consultants: Dr Anne Millard, BA Hons, Dip Ed, PhD

A CIP catalogue record for this book
is available from the British Library.

ISBN   0 7496 3879 6 (hbk)
        0 7496 4205 X (pbk)

Dewey Classification 942.05

Printed in Great Britain

CONTENTS

CHAPTER ONE
A New Game

Sir Francis Drake stared out of the tiny leaded windows on the forecastle of his ship. Below, on the deck, sailors sat in groups coiling ropes as thick as snakes into neat piles. Others greased and polished huge wooden blocks and pulleys.

They were getting ready to put to sea.

Or that was what he hoped.

Sir Francis sighed and rubbed a rough hand

over his high forehead. That was what he had hoped every day for the past month.

And every day, just as a messenger had arrived from the Queen giving him permission to sail, another one had come running behind to tell him the Queen had changed her mind again.

Sir Francis groaned. His gangplank was worn smooth with all the comings and goings.

"Godfrey, Earl Inkblot, to see you, Captain," squeaked his cabin boy.

"Send him up," growled Sir Francis.

Earl Inkblot was one of the Queen's advisors and Sir Francis had invited him to his cabin to discuss the Queen's orders.

Sir Francis turned and looked down at the rotten food that was spread over his oak table. There was a particularly nasty-looking lump of cheese, placed beside what had once been a loaf of bread and was now something purple and hairy.

Sir Francis wanted the Earl of Inkblot to see for himself what a waste the Queen created every time she changed her mind.

"Ugh!" cried Godfrey, Earl Inkblot, as he strode into the oak-panelled room. "What's that disgusting smell?"

"Lunch," said Sir Francis Drake. He held up a basket of rotten apples. "And this is for pudding!"

***

Queen Elizabeth I clutched a tiny wooden ship in her slender white hand. In front of her, lots of little ships bobbed about in a big tub of water.

Some looked like English ships with tiny English flags. Others looked like Spanish galleons with tiny Spanish flags. The Queen liked toys and games and was playing her favourite new game – *English Success at Sea.*

Opposite the Queen was Matilda, Lady Mouthwater. Water dripped down Lady Matilda's face. The front of her dress was soaked through and her hair hung like wet rope over her ears.

Behind Lady Matilda, Mary Marchbank stood with a silk blindfold in her hand. It was her job to cover one of the players' eyes when the battle was being fought at night.

TUDOR TOYS — SOMETHING FOR EVERYONE

Shake the Rattle

Spin the Top

Whirl the Hoop with a Stick

Catch the Ball in the Cup

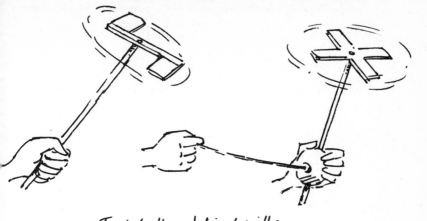

Twirl the Windmills

Ride the Hobby Horse

Faster you blockhead!

The Queen said it was more exciting that way. But since it was the Queen who made the rules (she always played with the English ships), it was always the other person who got attacked at night and had to wear the blindfold.

Somehow the Queen managed to sail in fine, clear weather twenty-four hours a day.

"Attack!" bellowed the Queen. A nasty gleam came into her eye. She nodded at Mary. "At night!"

Mary stepped forward and wrapped the blindfold over Matilda, Lady Mouthwater's eyes.

At the same moment, the Queen plunged her little English ship into the tub and rammed it into a fleet of tiny Spanish galleons.

A wave of water crashed over the edge of the tub and landed SPLOSH! Right in Lady Matilda's lap.

"Defend your position, you idiot!" shrieked the Queen. "Defend, or be defeated!"

Wave after wave of water splashed over the side of the tub.

Poor Lady Matilda!

How could she defend her position when she couldn't see anything? She felt her way gingerly along the edge of the tub. Her fingers grasped something sharp and wooden, sticking out of something else.

By the time she realised what it was, it was too late!

"Return cannon fire!" bellowed the Queen. She picked up a large pea shooter, aimed it over the tub and blew hard.

A shower of hard peas stung Matilda, Lady Mouthwater all over her face. BOP! An extra large, extra hard pea hit her right on the end of her nose.

It was the last straw. Matilda Lady Mouthwater burst into tears.

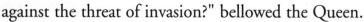

"Cry baby!" crowed the Queen. "You'll never make a sailor, will you?"

"Nooo," wailed Lady Mouthwater, "and I don't want to, either."

"Are you refusing to defend your country against the threat of invasion?" bellowed the Queen.

She whacked the tub with her hand. It was the same sort of noise that an executioner's axe made.

"That's treason!"

"It's NOT treason," wailed Lady Mouthwater. "It's only a GAME!"

As quickly as she could Mary Marchbank glided across the room towards the hearth. There was small shelf in the hearth wall. On it she kept a bowl of hot water and a huge bunch of marjoram.

Marjoram never failed to soothe the Queen if she became – what was the word? thought Mary, as she dumped the entire bunch of marjoram into the steaming water, ah, yes – overexcited.

Mary turned just in time to see the Queen tip the entire contents of the tub into Lady Matilda's lap.

"Traitor!" shrieked the Queen.

Yes, thought Mary. The Queen was definitely overexcited.

"Where am I?" gulped Lady Mouthwater, who was still blindfolded. "I can't swim!"

At that moment, the sweet smell of marjoram filled the room.

The Queen breathed deeply and sat back on her enormous chair. "What's that lovely smell?" she asked, sleepily.

"Your favourite marjoram," murmured Mary Marchbank. As she spoke, she quickly undid Lady Matilda's blindfold.

"Ah, marjoram," sighed the Queen. "We like marjoram."

Mary Marchbank saw her chance. "And the Lady Mouthwater?" she whispered soothingly.

"We don't like her," replied the Queen sleepily. "She's wet."

As quietly as she could, Mary opened the door and Matilda, Lady Mouthwater crawled out of the room on her hands and knees.

The Queen yawned and reached for her favourite cushion. It was embroidered with an English sailing ship. The figure of Sir Francis Drake stood on its deck.

"Mary?"

Mary curtseyed as low as she could. Surely the Queen would not want to speak to Matilda, Lady Mouthwater again?

"Yes, Your Majesty?" she said.

The Queen cuddled the cushion in her arms. "Tell Sir Francis we will be waiting for our story at teatime."

A puzzled look passed over Mary's face.

"But Your Majesty, don't you remember? You gave Sir Francis permission to put to sea yesterday."

The Queen smiled and a silly look came over her face.

"We changed our mind," she sniggered.

***

Sir Francis Drake banged his fist down on the heavy oak table. Stale buns and rotten apples bounced onto the floor.

"I am a ship's captain, Earl Inkblot!" he shouted. "My job is to protect the country not to tell teatime stories to the Queen."

Godfrey, Earl Inkblot, ducked as a loaf of hairy purple bread sailed past his ear. He took a deep breath and tried to stop his stomach rumbling.

Godfrey, Earl Inkblot, loved his food and missing lunch was a terrible disappointment to him.

"Leave it with me, Sir Francis," he muttered as a loud stomach rumble floated like a line of bubbles between them. "Don't worry, I'll sort it out."

"Do it quickly," growled Sir Francis Drake. "Or we'll be answering to the Spanish before the year is out."

❀ CHAPTER TWO ❀
The Queen's Toy Chest

Mary Marchbank stood in the doorway of Sydney
Woodshavings' workshop and breathed in the sharp
tangy smell of oak chips.

Mary loved the smell of oak chips because it
reminded her of Sydney, her sweetheart.

The workshop was empty but Mary's eyes
travelled to the bench where Sydney kept his tools
and chisels. Some were huge and blunt. Others were

tiny and as sharp
as razors. They were all
laid out in neat and
tidy rows.

Sydney could make
anything – big or small.
And whatever he made
was always perfect.

Mary sighed deeply
and small smile flickered
across her face. As far as
she was concerned
Sydney Woodshavings
was perfect, too.

It hardly seemed any
time at all since he had
moved from Crusty Castle to work for the Queen in
London. Indeed the Queen had been so delighted
with the bed Sydney had made her when she stayed
at Crusty Castle, she had immediately appointed
him Furniture Maker to the Royal Household.

Now Sydney had been given another honour.

The Queen had appointed him Toy Ship
Maker. And since then, Sydney had spent more and

more time using the tiny sharp chisels on his work bench to carve miniature ships for the Queen's collection.

He had even made her a toy chest that looked just like the sea chest Sir Francis Drake took with him on all his voyages. Except inside, instead of the compartments for rolled parchment orders and maps, the Queen's chest had rows of shelves for all her toy ships.

And each ship had its own special place.

Mary knew this better than anyone.

Every afternoon she had to polish each ship and put it away. Then the Queen had to see for herself that everything was 'ship shape' before the chest could be closed.

Mary looked again at the woodcarver's bench with its rows of tools and chisels. Maybe one day, Sydney would have a bench like that in his own little cottage. And maybe in the same little cottage, Mary would have a row of wooden spoons and kitchen knives.

"Farthing for your thoughts," murmured Sydney Woodshavings in her ear.

Mary jumped. "Sydney!" she gasped. "I didn't hear you!"

Sydney's brown eyes twinkled. "But I saw you," he said. He bent down and kissed Mary on the cheek.

Mary blushed and turned away. "I was thinking about a little cottage," she murmured.

Sydney grinned. "I think of that cottage all the time."

"If only the Queen would make up her

mind and let us marry," said Mary. As she spoke, she remembered the piece of paper in her pocket.

The Queen had given it to her with orders to show it to Sydney immediately. It was a drawing of a Dutch galleon. They were a different shape from the English and the Spanish ships.

The Queen wanted six of them carved by the end of the week.

Now it was Sydney's turn to sigh. He had been making the toy ships in his spare time in the hope that the Queen might finally reward him with permission to marry Mary Marchbank.

But as each day went by, the Queen wanted more and more ships and it was getting more and more difficult to find the time.

For the past week, Sydney Woodshavings had been up most nights putting the final touches to the little ships. He even rigged them with string and tiny cotton sails that Mary made.

The problem was that once the Queen wanted something, woe betide the servant who did not deliver it.

BATTLING IT OUT — FIGHTING SHIPS

English ships were smaller, faster and had better guns.

"I hear Sir Francis Drake was refused permission to sail again," said Sydney, as he looked at the piece of paper with the drawing. "If he didn't tell such good stories, the Queen would have let him sail long ago."

Mary nodded. She knew only too well that apart from playing *English Sucesses at Sea*, the Queen only wanted to do one other thing.

And that was to listen to Sir Francis Drake tell stories of his voyages to the West Indies.

It seemed the Queen just couldn't get enough of

tales of palm-fringed islands, strange tribes, exotic fruit and, best of all, stories of clumsy Spanish galleons, loaded to the decks with treasure that got captured in the night.

And it wasn't just the stories the Queen liked. On one of Sir Francis' early trips, she had lent him money in return for a share of stolen treasure.

Three years later, when he returned with his pockets bulging with gold, Sir Francis Drake paid her back a thousand times as much as she had given him in the first place!

And everyone knew the Queen's views on money.

She liked lots of it!

There was a sound of footsteps approaching across the cobbled yard.

Sydney Woodshavings pulled a face. "If that's another order from the Queen, I'm just going to have to say no!"

CHAPTER THREE
A Suspicious Recipe

The door opened and Toby Crumble came in with a covered basket over his arm.

"Toby!" cried Mary. She smiled and kissed him quickly on the cheek. "Thank goodness, it's you!"

Toby Crumble was a cook in the Queen's kitchen. He had known Mary and Sydney for a long time and they were all good friends. Indeed they often met at Sydney's workshop for a gossip and sometimes Toby brought a few pies from the kitchen's great larders.

Sydney Woodshavings lifted a corner of the cloth that covered Toby's basket. "Mmm!" He sniffed deeply. "Chicken and Leek, my favourite!"

Sydney cleared a space on his workbench and Toby set up the pies and a flagon of mild beer.

There were even some candied fruits left over from a banquet the week before.

As they ate, Mary recounted the story of the Queen's new game. "Poor Lady Mouthwater always has to be the Spanish navy!" she giggled.

Suddenly Toby went white and put down his half -finished pie.

"Toby!" cried Mary. She rested her hand on his arm. "Is something the matter?"

For a moment, Toby didn't reply. Then he took a deep breath. "I've been worrying since last week.

I've got to get it off my chest. Something's the matter," he said. "And it could be very important."

Then Toby explained how there had been a big banquet in honour of the Spanish Ambassador only the week before.

"I prepared the stuffed swans and the pigs'

heads," said Toby. "And the Spanish ambassador sent Greedy Gonzalez over to make the candied fruits and jellies."

"Who's Greedy Gonzalez?" asked Sydney. He chewed on a sugar apricot.

Whoever this Gonzalez was, he certainly knew how to make tasty candied fruits.

Toby shrugged. "He's a kind of friend. We've known each other for ages. Sometimes we help each other out and swap recipes."

Then Toby explained how it had taken two or three days to prepare all the food so Greedy Gonzalez had stayed overnight in the servants' quarters so that the two of them could start work at dawn.

Sydney Woodshavings pulled a face. "There doesn't seem anything wrong in that."

"There isn't," said Toby. "What's worrying me is what Greedy told me after we'd finished cooking and he'd swallowed a flagon of ale."

By the time Toby had told them what he heard, both Mary Marchbank and Sydney Woodshavings had gone pale, too.

Greedy Gonzalez said a new Spanish chef called Alfonzo had arrived at the Ambassador's house. "I no like heem one leetle bit." Greedy Gonzalez had muttered. "He ees nasty and mean."

Then Greedy Gonzalez had drunk another mug of beer and told Toby how Alfonzo had boasted about a huge farewell supper he had cooked for thousands of sailors about to put to sea.

He'd used their normal ship's rations of fish, oil, rice and wine and turned it into a feast.

Then Alfonzo had fixed Greedy Gonzalez with a spiteful look. Only a genius like me could have done it, Alfonzo had declared. Not a pan scrubber like you.

"I no pan scrubber!" Greedy Gonzalez had wailed at Toby. A great big, beery tear had rolled down his cheek. "I a brilliant cook like my friend, Toby."

For a moment Sydney Woodshaving's workshop was silent. Toby and Mary and Sydney looked at each other. It didn't take a genius to work out that if thousands of Spanish sailors were eating a farewell supper, then something suspicious was afoot.

After all, Spain had been threatening to make war on England at any moment, so thousands of Spanish sailors could only mean an invasion by sea.

"What shall I do?" cried Toby. "Maybe Greedy Gonzalez was exaggerating? Maybe it was hundreds not thousands?"

Sydney Woodshavings looked serious. "If you tell the Queen and you're wrong, she will call it treachery."

"And if you don't tell her and you're right," muttered Mary. "She'll call it treason."

Toby stuffed the last of the cold pie into his mouth. It was comforting somehow.

"What am I going to do?" he said, again.

Suddenly the image of a woman floated into Mary's mind. She looked like a bloated squirrel and she lived in hovel that made a pigsty look clean. But when there was a problem, she always knew how to solve it.

"I'll talk to Old Ma Knucklebone," said Mary firmly. "She'll tell us what to do."

CHAPTER FOUR
Good Advice

Old Ma Knucklebone knew exactly what to do. She wiped her face with a greasy cloth and put on her best cap with the lucky foxtail.

"Come along, lass," she said, as she steered Mary into the busy street. "We're off to the port, you and me."

Mary took one last look at the cave-like hovel. There were animal skins and bunches of feathers on the wall. A filthy kettle still steamed gently over a low fire.

Mary shuddered. Nothing had changed since her first visit. And even back then, Old Ma Knucklebone had saved the day.

Mary wrapped her cloak tightly around her shoulders. She hoped the advice she was taking now would be just as good.

Old Ma Knucklebone cackled as she shoved the cat out of the way and kicked the door shut.

"'Course it will, dear," she said.

Mary gasped. It was as if the old woman was reading her mind!

Old Ma Knucklebone threw back her head and cackled louder than ever.

"'Course I am," she said.

***

In the oak-panelled cabin on board his ship, Sir Francis Drake smelled his visitors before he actually saw them.

A smell something like a mixture of dead fox and camel droppings seeped in underneath his door.

Sir Francis Drake looked again at the coded message that lay on his table. It was from a servant of the Queen, who said she would be paying him a visit.

It said that dangerous rumours were floating around. Rumours that Sir Francis needed to hear in person. The servant would be bringing an advisor.

Sir Francis' nose twitched involuntarily as he stared across the cabin floor.

At that moment, the cabin boy opened the door. His face was green and he was holding his nose. "Ugh, uh –"

"Send them in, boy," muttered Sir Francis.

A young woman with a heart shaped face and eyes like shiny chestnuts glided into the room. She curtseyed and introduced herself as Mary Marchbank, maid to the Queen.

Sir Francis bowed. He would never have believed such a pretty girl could be so smelly.

A second figure clomped in behind her. She had a face like a bloated squirrel and her filthy grey dress was covered in green stains and crusty yellow lumps. A foxtail hung from the greasy cap on her head.

"Old Ma Knucklebone at your service, Sir," she said with a toothy grin that revealed her rotting teeth. She stood by the only open window. "If you don't mind, I'll stand 'ere." Old Ma Knucklebone patted her middle. "I gets queasy on the water."

As if they couldn't help themselves, Mary Marchbank and Sir Francis Drake exchanged looks of pure panic.

The prospect of Old Ma Knucklebone being queasy was terrifying.

Mary curtseyed. "Allow me to tell you everything I know, Sir Francis," she said quickly.

Sir Francis pulled out a chair as fast as he could. "Go ahead," he almost shouted.

Ten minutes later, Sir Francis Drake drew his brows together and laid down his pen. What Mary had told him was serious. Very serious indeed.

Because it was exactly the same as the information he had received only that morning from one of his own network of spies.

The Spanish were putting together a huge fleet of boats. And its sole purpose was the invasion of England!

Sir Francis clenched his hand into a tight fist. How on earth could he protect his country, if the Queen wouldn't let him put to sea?

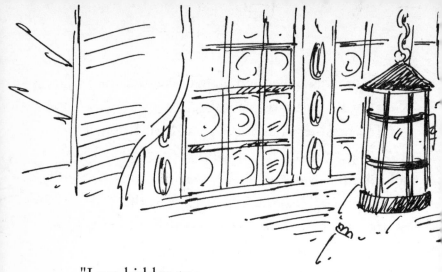

"I am bidden to
see your mistress, this afternoon," he
muttered. "Perhaps she will finally grant me
permission to sail."

Mary's eyes were round and worried. Only that
morning, the Queen had mentioned how much she
was looking forward to hearing Sir Francis' new
story. She had even told Mary that the story had
three parts.

And that Sir Francis had promised to tell it over
three days.

"I fear you will not be successful, Sir,"
murmured Mary. And then she explained why.

"What am I going to do?" wailed Sir Francis.
Mary looked up. His voice sounded just like Toby
Crumble's.

"That's why you needs my advice, Your
Captainess," squawked Old Ma Knucklebone. She
crossed the cabin and untied a leather pouch that hung
from her belt. "The bones never lie."

Sir Francis Drake watched in amazement as Old
Ma Knucklebone grabbed a handful of dirty little
bones and scattered them all over his desk.

He opened his mouth to protest. The stink was
unbelievable. Old Ma Knucklebone held up her hand.

"I knows you can't wait for worrying," she said.

She reached into her pocket and pulled out a piece of grey gristle. "I needs time to study the bones." As she popped the gristle into her mouth, both Mary Marchbank and Sir Francis leapt to the open window, clutching their stomachs.

Five minutes later, Old Ma Knucklebone scooped up the little bones and dropped them into her leather pouch.

"One sovereign, Your Captainess," she said, holding out a grimy hand.

"One sovereign?" cried Sir Francis Drake. "But you haven't told me anything."

"'Course I haven't," cackled Old Ma Knucklebone. "But I wills when you pays me."

And that was when she told Sir Francis that she

had seen two things in the bones. A terrible story and a pretty monkey.

Sir Francis stared at the beady-eyed hag standing in front of him. He had never heard such nonsense in all of his life. He had half a mind to have her thrown overboard.

At least it might sort out the smell! But at that moment there was a knock on the door.

"Bosun Grundy to see you, Sir," called the cabin boy.

Behind the door came the sound of high-pitched chattering.

Sir Francis Drake frowned. Bosun Grundy had just returned from a voyage to South America.

When he had left, two years ago, he had spoken with a thick Devon accent. Now he sounded like some sort of primitive!

"Send him in," called Sir Francis.

The door opened and a wiry young man walked into the room.

Sir Francis Drake gasped.

Mary clapped her hands over her mouth.

Old Ma Knucklebone burst out laughing.

Sitting on Bosun Grundy's shoulders was a bright-eyed, golden-haired monkey. It wore a little purple hat and had a ruff around its neck.

Bosun Grundy grinned. "Pretty, ain't it?" he said.

CHAPTER FIVE
A Pretty Monkey

Sir Francis Drake stood outside the Queen's chamber. He had to admit Old Ma Knucklebone's plan was ingenious.

The first thing he needed to do was make his story really, really boring. Then, when the Queen threw him out, he would send her the pretty monkey as an apology.

"Mark my words, Your Captainess," Old Ma

Knucklebone had cackled. "She'll be too busy playing with the monkey to want another story from you."

"But will she let me sail?" Sir Francis had asked.

"You'll be away on the evening tide," Old Ma Knucklebone had answered.

"Her Majesty is waiting," said a soft voice.

Sir Francis blinked. For a moment he had forgotten where he was. Mary Marchbank smiled shyly. "Good luck," she whispered.

***

The Queen yawned and made irritating ripping noises with a small pair of scissors. Her favourite sailing ship cushion was in shreds.

"And then what happened?" she snapped.

"We got wet," replied Sir Francis in a stupid voice.

"But the sea, the sea," cried the Queen. "What was it like?"

"It was wet, too."

"What else?"

By now the Queen's voice was low and menacing and her temper was wearing thin.She had never been so bored in her life.

If this was the best Sir Francis could do, she would send him packing immediately.

"What else?" she repeated angrily.

"It was salty."

The Queen lost her temper. "Get out!" she yelled throwing the tattered cushion at Sir Francis.

"You're boring, stupid and dull!"

Sir Francis stood up and bowed.

So far so good.

Now it time to put the second part of the plan into action.

Two hours later, Sir Francis Drake carried a large heavy box up the great oak stairs to the Queen's chamber.

It was strange looking box. It was made out of wood and had holes in one end. The wood smelled salty and fruity as if the box had come a long way or from a foreign place.

Drake smiled to himself. It smelled exactly the same as the day it arrived in his cabin.

There was a rustle of skirts. Mary Marchbank appeared out of the shadows. Her face was white. Ever since her terrible teatime story, the Queen had been in a filthy temper. Not even a bowl of soothing marjoram had helped.

Now everything hinged on Old Ma
Knucklebone's plan and sometimes even Ma
Knucklebone didn't get things right first time.

"Do you have it with you, Sir?" whispered
Mary to Sir Francis.

Sir Francis's blue eyes glittered. "I do, my dear."

Mary took a deep breath and knocked.

"What?" yelled the Queen.

"Sir Francis Drake to see you again, Your
Majesty."

"What for?" yelled the Queen.

Sir Francis Drake bit his lip. "I have a, uh,
special delivery for you, Madam."

Five minutes later, the Queen was cooing and chuckling like a turtle dove. Her eyes shone like candles and there was huge grin across her face.

The box was open on the floor in front of her. A little monkey sat on the top of it.

Even Mary felt her insides go all gooey.

Sir Francis had dressed the little monkey in courtier's clothes. It even had a miniature sword.

Sir Francis bowed. "I trust my uh, special delivery meets with your approval," he muttered.

"He's booootiful," gushed the Queen. She picked up the monkey and held him in the air like a baby.

"We'll make you lots and lots of lovely clothes, sweetest one!" She nuzzled the monkey's ear. "We'll build a little house all for you!"

"Mary!" she yelled.

Mary Marchbank curtseyed. "Yes, Your Majesty."

"Send for Sydney Woodshavings immediately."

"Yes, Your Majesty."

The Queen chewed her lip as if another thought had just occurred to her.

"Oh, and, Sir Francis –?"

The Queen rocked the monkey like a baby and planted a kiss on top of his head. "You may sail on the evening tide."

"Thank you, Your Majesty," said Sir Francis.

Sir Francis turned and walked towards the heavy oak doors. A smug smile played on his lips.

Everything had gone like clockwork. Indeed it all seemed so simple now, that he couldn't think why he had relied on that smelly hag, Old Ma Knucklebone, in the first place.

Or indeed why he had paid her a sovereign of his own money!

Next time he had trouble with the Queen, he'd sort it out himself!

At that moment, there was a thin nasty noise.

It was the Queen sniggering.

"On second thoughts Sir Francis," she murmured. "I think I'll change my mind –"

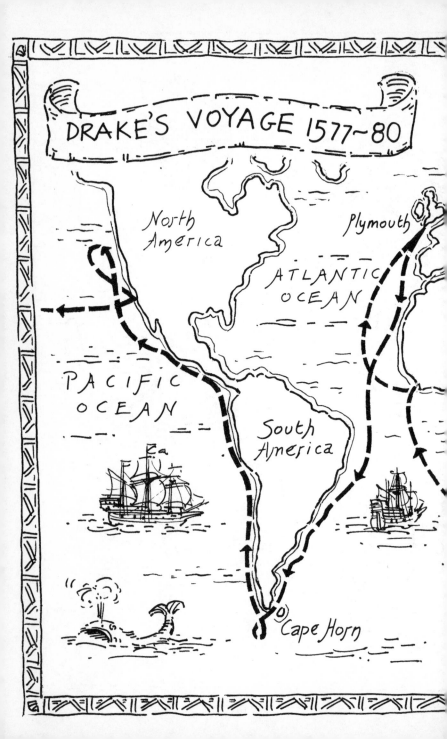

DRAKE'S VOYAGE 1577~80

North America

Plymouth

ATLANTIC OCEAN

PACIFIC OCEAN

South America

Cape Horn

❀ NOTES ❀
At the Court of Queen Elizabeth
(How it really was!)

Elizabethan Toys

In Elizabethan times, children were dressed like adults and expected to behave like adults from a very early age.

However, whilst they still could, children played 'cup and ball' and 'rolling the hoop', which were also forms of exercise. Hobby horses, toy ships, soldiers and drums were also popular. Wooden toys, including dolls, were imported from Holland and Germany and were rarer. Rich children were given rattles made of silver.

Elizabethan Dockyards

The wealth of the Elizabethan era was largely due to the trading links created by Elizabeth's merchant shipping fleets.

Because of this, in the late 1580's, a dockyard was an extremely busy place. For the first time there was direct trade between England and the Baltic and further south with the Levant and the wool and spices trade was especially profitable.

The English navel fleet was also well maintained and always ready at anchor. The sailors came from all parts of society but many were forced to join by special agents who visited taverns late at night and signed up unsuspecting drinkers.

Drake's Voyage around the World

Sir Francis Drake sailed around the world between 1577 and 1580. His ship was called The Golden Hind.

Elizabeth I had given Sir Francis orders to explore new territories and steal as much gold as possible. On his way back through the Spice Islands, he added six tonnes of cloves to his store of treasure. However, Sir Francis struck a reef and had to throw most of the cloves overboard.

On his return, the Queen attended a special banquet on his ship and many presents were made for her from the emeralds and diamonds he had stolen from other ships.

Spanish Galleons

Spanish Galleons were huge, heavy and difficult to manoeuvre. They usually had four masts and their guns were clumsy and slow to reload.

In addition, Spanish sailors were not as highly-trained as English sailors. Indeed, many had no knowledge of the sea at all.

Food aboard these galleons was said to be worse than the food on the English ships and the rations smaller.

English Fighting Ships

English ships were much smaller than Spanish galleons, which meant they could move faster and do more damage.

Another big difference was that the English ships were built to capture their enemy using gunfire.

When the Spanish and English ships fought, the Spanish could never get near enough to board the English ships but the English were able to use their superior gunfire.